10
Minute Tales

Timmy Helps a Friend

When you see these symbols:

Read aloud
Read aloud to
your child.

Read alone
Support your child
as they read alone.

Read along
Read along with
your child.

EGMONT
We bring stories to life

At Nursery it was Stripey's birthday.
In the Courtyard, Osbourne put down a
cardboard box full of things to play with.
Hoot! Hoot!

The class gathered around the box.
What could be inside? Timmy stood on his
tiptoes and peeked over the top.
Baah! Baah!

It is Stripey's birthday. Timmy wants to help Stripey have lots of fun.

Read aloud   Read along

Timmy spotted a beanbag inside the box.
Baah! He picked it up and threw it to
Yabba. **Quack! Quack!**

Timmy was pleased – he loved playing catch!
Finlay joined in too. Soon everyone was playing,
except for the birthday badger.

Stripey was sad. He didn't know how to
play catch. **Honk! Honk!**

Read alone

Timmy plays catch with Yabba and Finlay.
But poor Stripey does not know how to play.

Read aloud   Read along

Timmy didn't want Stripey to be upset on his birthday, so he showed him how to play catch. **Baah! Baah!**

But, **plop!** Every time Timmy threw the beanbag, Stripey missed it.

Stripey honked sadly. It was no use; he just couldn't catch.

Timmy was sad too. He wanted to help Stripey join in all the fun.

Timmy shows Stripey how to play catch.
But Stripey keeps dropping the beanbag.
He is very sad.

Perhaps Stripey would be better at a different game? The friends went into the garden to play with a football.

Timmy carefully put some paint tins one on top of the other to make a tower. The friends then took turns kicking and throwing the football at the tins. They were trying to knock the tower down!

Stripey couldn't wait for his go!
Honk! Honk!

Read alone

Next, the friends play a ball game.
Stripey gets very excited!

Read aloud **Read along**

Finally, it was Stripey's turn. He was sure this would be a fun game.

Stripey took a deep breath. He ran towards the football and kicked it. **Thump!**

But the football missed the tower and flew over the Nursery fence. **Crash!**

Stripey sat down. He couldn't play ball or catch. What was he going to do?

Read alone

Stripey joins in with the ball game but he is not very good. Poor Stripey.

Timmy grabbed Stripey's hand and pulled him up. Timmy had an idea!
Baah! Baah!

Timmy took a tennis ball, a flowerpot and a knobbly stick from Osbourne's box. The aim of the game was to hit the ball into the pot.

Stripey grinned. This was it! He could finally join in with the birthday fun. He waited while Otus had his turn. Stripey was so excited!
Honk! Honk!

Read alone

Timmy thinks of another game to play.
Stripey cannot wait to try it!

Stripey clapped and honked when Otus hit the ball into the pot. Now it was his turn to play! He took the knobbly stick, and hit the ball. **Thwack!**

But Stripey hit the ball too hard. It went flying into the sky and disappeared.

Stripey picked up the flowerpot just to check, but the ball wasn't in there. He honked sadly. This wasn't a very fun birthday.

Timmy was worried. He had to think of another game for Stripey to try.

Read alone

But Stripey is not very good at the next game either. Stripey is very sad.

Read aloud Read along

Just then, Timmy heard a
Boing! Boing!

He stood on his tiptoes and looked over
the gate. Yabba was playing with a bat
and ball! Timmy led Stripey over. This was
the fun game they were looking for!

The friends were so excited. **Baah! Quack!
Honk!** At last Stripey was going to be part
of the fun.

Yabba picked up the ball and bounced it to
Stripey. Stripey watched the ball carefully,
ready to bounce it to Timmy ...

Read alone

Yabba is playing bat and ball. Timmy and Stripey want to play too.

Read aloud Read along

But Stripey missed, and the ball fell on the ground. **Plop!**

They tried again. And again. But every time Stripey tried to bounce the ball on his bat, he missed.

Yabba was frustrated. **Quack! Quack!** Stripey couldn't play the game!

Then the Cuckoo Clock called the class in for Art Time. Stripey slowly shuffled inside.

Read alone

But Stripey cannot play bat and ball very well either. The class go inside for Art Time.

Inside, the class sat down at the art tables. They made paper hats and cards for Stripey's birthday.

Ba**ah!** bleated Timmy, showing his hat to Stripey. Timmy was sure it would cheer him up. But Stripey was still sad. He just wanted to play a ball game with his friends.

Timmy wanted to help Stripey. But what could he do?

The class make paper hats. But Stripey only wants to play with his friends.

Soon it was time for the class to colour in their birthday cards. Osbourne took a rubber band off a bundle of coloured pencils.

Ping!

The rubber band flew through the air and landed on a bat and ball. Timmy picked up the rubber band and stretched it. Then Timmy had an idea. He knew how to help Stripey!

Baah! Baah!

Read alone

Timmy has an idea. He knows how to help Stripey join in!

Read aloud **Read along**

While the rest of the class coloured in their cards, Osbourne and Harriet helped Timmy with his idea.

Osbourne snipped the rubber band in half and tied one end around the ball. Harriet tied the other end to the bat.

Timmy tried out his bat, ball and rubber band invention. He stretched the ball and let it go ... **Boing! Boing!** The ball bounced on the bat. Timmy couldn't wait to show Stripey.

Baah! Baah!

Harriet and Osbourne help Timmy with his idea. They tie a bat and ball together with a rubber band.

The clock rang out for Play Time, **Cuckoo Cuckoo!** The class ran into the playground.

Yabba, Finlay and Otus played bat and ball, and Ruffy, Apricot and Paxton ran off to play football.

Stripey stood all by himself, watching. He couldn't get the hang of any of the games. This was the worst birthday ever! **Honk! Honk!**

Read alone

It is Play Time and all of the class play games together. Poor Stripey is left out.

Read aloud   **Read along**

Just then, Timmy rushed into the playground. He gave Stripey his bat and ball invention. **Baah!** bleated Timmy. Happy Birthday, Stripey!

Stripey scratched his head. What was this? **Honk! Honk!**

Timmy showed Stripey what to do and watched as his friend gave it a try.

Stripey lifted up the ball and ... **Boing! Boing!** It bounced on the bat, hooray! He practised and practised, bouncing the ball faster and faster.

Read alone

Timmy gives Stripey the bat and ball tied together with the rubber band. Stripey practises very hard.

Read aloud   Read along

Stripey practised so much that soon he could bounce the ball without the rubber band! Then he could play a game of bat and ball with Timmy.

Timmy was very happy. He had helped Stripey enjoy his birthday! The whole class cheered and clapped.

Yip yap! Toowit toowoo! Quack! Quack! Baah! Baah!

Stripey grinned. It was a great birthday, after all! **Honk! Honk!**

Now he can do it! At last, Stripey can play
with his friends. Happy Birthday, Stripey!

Timmy time

Have fun with Timmy with this

BAA-RILLIANT APP!

Everyone's favourite little lamb now has his very own iPad app

Available on the **App Store**

Just £2.99!

★ Two stories narrated by actress Josie Lawrence bring Timmy, Paxton, Yabba, Otus and Mittens to life.

★ Full of fun & noisy sound effects that kids will love.

★ Touch Bumpy the Caterpillar to reveal hidden clips from the TV show.

★ Play tunes with a Timmy twist on the keyboard!

★ Colouring pages to keep little hands out of mischief.

An entertaining and engaging app that supports both language and literacy development that is great fun too!